The Nutcracker

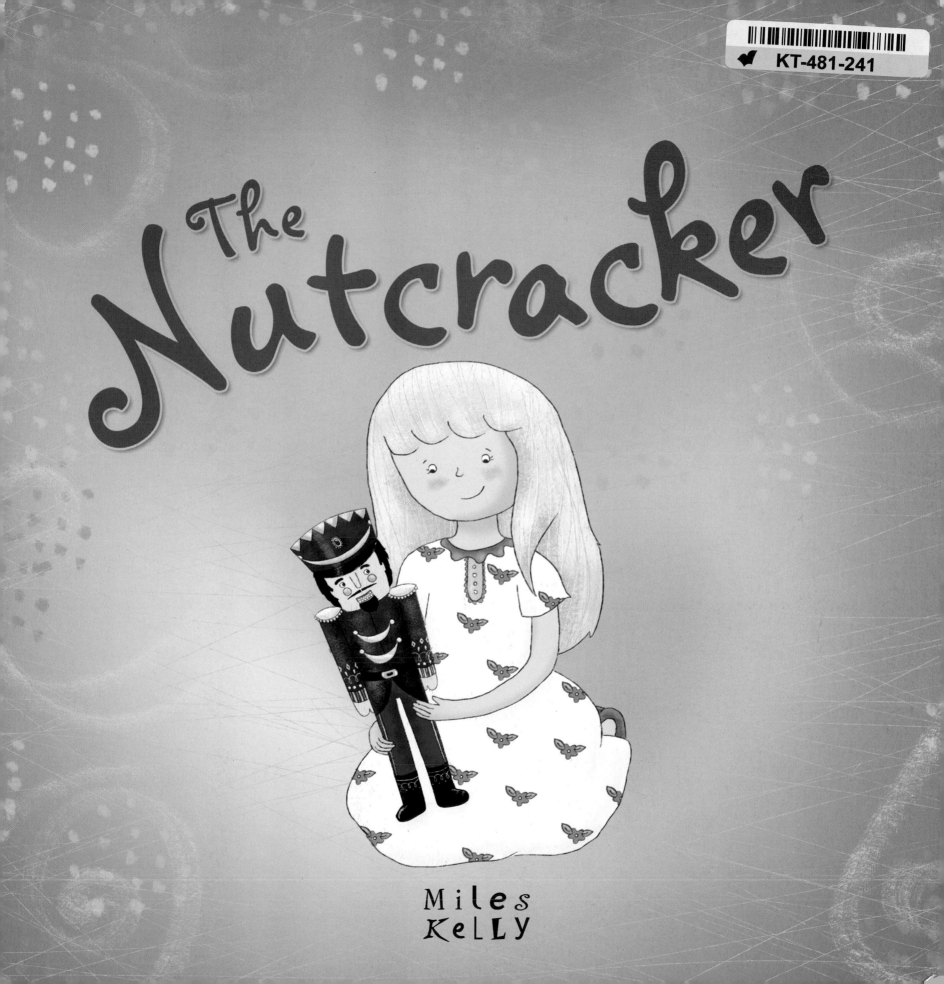

Miles
Kelly

It was Christmas Eve, and Clara was
staring out of the window at the snow
falling on to the icy ground outside.

Inside, the Christmas party was starting. Everything looked **twinkly** and **magical**. Clara's brother, Franz, and her cousins ran around excitedly.

Suddenly Clara's godfather appeared. He was a toymaker and he always made the children beautiful toys. "Merry Christmas!" he cried and handed presents to all the children.

To Clara he gave the best present of all. "He's a very special nutcracker," whispered Clara's godfather.

The Nutcracker looked like a toy soldier, but he could crack nuts with his teeth. Franz tried to crack a huge walnut, but suddenly the Nutcracker's jaw snapped!

CRACK!

Clara began to cry. "Don't worry," said her godfather, tying his handkerchief around the Nutcracker's jaw. "I'll mend him properly in the morning."

Soon it was time for bed. Clara laid her
Nutcracker under the tree with the
other toys, but she couldn't sleep
thinking about her broken toy.

Clara crept downstairs, and snuggled down next to the tree with her Nutcracker. She quickly fell asleep.

Suddenly, there was a loud creaking sound! Clara woke to find the Nutcracker and the toy soldiers had grown.
"Hello, I'm the Nutcracker Prince," he said, bowing to Clara.

"I'm here to protect you," said the Nutcracker Prince. Clara heard a scuttling sound and a mouse army crept out of the shadows.

Immediately, the toy soldiers and the Nutcracker Prince drew their swords. With a loud squeak, the Mouse King charged and the battle began.

"I have to help," said Clara. Amid the shouts and clanging of swords, Clara took off a slipper and threw it at the Mouse King.

The Mouse King fell to the ground. There was a moment of silence, then the other mice scuttled away.

Clara stared in amazement as the Nutcracker became a handsome Prince.

"Your bravery broke the Mouse King's spell," said the Prince. "I've been trapped as a toy for years, but now I'm free!" The Prince handed Clara the Mouse King's crown.

"We must celebrate!" said the Prince as he called for his magical sleigh and reindeer. Clara's nightgown turned into a beautiful ballgown.

The Prince and Clara flew through the air
in the sleigh. They sailed through the snowy night
until they reached the Land of Sweets.

Soon the sleigh came to a stop in front of a castle. A Sugar Plum Fairy was waiting for them.

"Welcome to the Marzipan Palace!" she said.

The Prince told the
Sugar Plum Fairy
how Clara had saved him.
"We must have a banquet
in your honour," she cried,
clapping her hands.

The banquet was astounding. There were cakes, cookies, sweets and fancies from every corner of the world.

As they feasted, dancers from every country whirled and pranced, leapt and jumped. Clara stared in amazement.

All too soon it was time for the final dance. The Prince and the Sugar Plum Fairy walked to the centre of the floor and performed a

magnificent waltz.

Clara thought they looked **beautiful**. She curled up in her chair to watch the dancers and the flecks of light moving with them. Slowly, Clara's eyes began to close.

When Clara woke up she was at home again, under the Christmas tree. The Prince was gone, but her nutcracker toy was lying in her arms, his jaw fixed into a knowing smile.